For Tony: I love you more than tacos —T.V.

For María and Guadalupe —J.M.

Text copyright © 2019 by Tanya Valentine
Jacket art and interior illustrations copyright © 2019 by Jorge Martin

All rights reserved. Published in the United States by Schwartz & Wade Books, an imprint of
Random House Children's Books, a division of Penguin Random House LLC, New York.

Schwartz & Wade Books and the colophon are trademarks of Penguin Random House LLC.

Visit us on the Web! rhcbooks.com

Educators and librarians, for a variety of teaching tools, visit us at RHTeachersLibrarians.com

Library of Congress Cataloging-in-Publication Data
Names: Valentine, Tanya, author. | Martin, Jorge (Illustrator), illustrator.
Title: Little Taco Truck / by Tanya Valentine ; illustrated by Jorge Martin.
Description: First edition. | New York : Schwartz & Wade Books, [2018] | Summary: Little Taco Truck loves serving workers on Union Street,
but when Ms. Falafal takes his spot, then more and bigger food trucks arrive, he fears no one will want his tacos anymore.
Identifiers: LCCN 2017037017 (print) | LCCN 2017049465 (ebook) | ISBN 978-1-5247-6587-3 (ebk) | ISBN 978-1-5247-6585-9 (trade) | ISBN 978-1-5247-6586-6 (glb)
Subjects: | CYAC: Food trucks—Fiction. | Cooperativeness—Fiction.
Classification: LCC PZ7.1.V343 (ebook) | LCC PZ7.1.V343 Lit 2018 (print) | DDC [E]—dc23

The text of this book is set in Deccan.
The illustrations were rendered digitally.
Book design by Rachael Cole

MANUFACTURED IN CHINA
2 4 6 8 10 9 7 5 3 1
First Edition

LITTLE TACO TRUCK

WRITTEN BY
TANYA VALENTINE
&
ILLUSTRATED BY
JORGE MARTIN

schwartz & wade books · new york

In a busy corner of the big city,
new buildings began to rise.

And each day Little Taco Truck loved serving up tasty tacos to the hungry workers on Union Street.

But one day when Little Taco Truck arrived, he was surprised to see another truck parked in his spot.

"*Hola,* Miss Fal ... Fal ..." Little Taco Truck tried to sound out the words on the side of the other truck.

"Falafel," she said, smiling.

"Are you lost?" he asked.

"Oh, no," Miss Falafel said. "I'm here to serve delicious falafel sandwiches."

The smell of her fresh-baked pita bread and crunchy chickpea fritters floated through the air.

Little Taco Truck's engine rumbled.

He knew he should share his street.

But what if people love falafel more than tacos? he worried.

He secretly hoped Miss Falafel would find a street of her own the next day.

But the next day, Miss Falafel was parked in his space again. And . . . she had brought friends.

Little Taco Truck crept down the
street, looking for a place to park.

"Get your gumbo!" whooped Jumbo Gumbo.

"Gumbo?" Little Taco Truck shouted.

"Of course!" Jumbo Gumbo said. "Only a big truck like me can handle the big flavor of spicy Cajun seafood stew!"

Little Taco Truck's tires sagged. *How will people even see a little truck like me next to all these big trucks?* he worried.

"If you need a place to park," Jumbo Gumbo shouted, "look behind Annie!"

Little Taco Truck inched up the street toward
a brand-new bright yellow truck.
"Are you Annie?" he asked.

"Annie's Arepas," she said, sparkling in the sunlight. "Everyone loves my warm corn-bread sandwiches!"

Little Taco Truck sighed. *What if no one notices me next to a shiny new truck like Annie?*

The next day, even more food trucks lined
Union Street. Little Taco Truck tried to squeeze
into the last tiny space, when . . .

HELLO GELATO

"Ouch!" a big pink truck shouted.

"I'm sorry," Little Taco Truck said. "The street is so

crowded with falafel and gumbo and arepas and . . .

Hello Gelato?" He read the side of the truck.

"*Fantastico!*" Hello Gelato said.

"No! Not fantastic!" Little Taco Truck cried.

Little Taco Truck swished his wipers to hide his

tears as he drove away.

On his way home, he hatched a plan.

If I get to the city first, he thought, *no one can take*

my parking spot.

So in the dark of night, Little Taco Truck returned to the quiet city, parked in his favorite spot, and fell sound asleep.

In the bright light of day, he was startled awake as the other trucks arrived.

Working up his courage, Little Taco Truck blinked his lights, puffed up his tires, and said,

"This is *my* spot!"

"I'm sorry we didn't make room for you yesterday,
Little Taco Truck," said Miss Falafel.

"Me too," said Annie. "We can all fit if we squeeze.
I can move my tables onto the sidewalk."

"And I can move my signs out of the way!"

Jumbo Gumbo shouted.

Hello Gelato cheered when he arrived.

"You found the perfect spot!"

"I did!" Little Taco Truck happily tooted his horn. "It was right here all along."

And when Oodles of Noodles arrived the next day,

they made room for her, too.

GLOSSARY

arepa (a-RE-pa): This flat cake made of ground corn is one of the most popular foods in Colombia.

falafel (fa-LA-fel): A Middle Eastern dish of deep-fried balls made from spiced mashed chickpeas.

gelato (je-LA-to): A soft, rich Italian ice cream usually flavored with fruit, nuts, or cocoa powder.

gumbo (GUM-bo): This meat and shellfish stew is often served on top of rice and is the official dish of the state of Louisiana.

taco (TA-co): A crispy Mexican corn pancake folded or rolled around a filling of meat, beans, and cheese.

tapa (TA-pa): A small, savory Spanish dish served as an appetizer or a meal.